KEY LISTENER PUBLISHING

Written by: Michael and Lauren Quick

ISBN 978-1-105-46176-7

If you would like permission to use material from this book, please contact info@keylistener.com

First Edition: July 2021

Published by Key Listener Publishing
keylistenerpublishing.com
Bozeman, Montana, USA

*To Mothers everywhere,
the ultimate essential worker.*

Have you ever wondered aloud all it is that mommies do?

Well, look no further, my dear. Just turn the pages and let me tell you...

Some mommies have the job of teaching everyone.

We should always be learning, it is so very fun!

Look!

A mommy who wears a badge.
She keeps our streets safe and sound.

Our world would be a dangerous
place if she was not around.

This mommy works in the hospital to take care of people that are sick.

She uses different medicine to make her patients feel better quick!

"Look at this!" says this Mommy who designs.

Cars and boats and things that fly.

She is always reaching for the stars, just like buildings that scrape the sky.

Did you know there are mommies who make sure rules are followed and fair?

If you want to argue with these mommies, you had better prepare.

Some mommies stay at home
to keep our families at their best.

They do so much to keep all in
order, for that we are impressed!

In the boardroom this Mommy says, "Please allow me to explain..."

She amazes with her skillful presentation about the importance of supply chain.

Beep Beep!

This mommy drives a big truck to get things here and there.

She is always right on time with just a moment to spare.

We say "be safe" to the mommies who travel the globe to keep our nation safe and free.

We owe them much respect, for all they sacrifice for you and me.

We all share a mother, just not by birth.

She allows us to live, breathe, and play, her name is Mother Earth.

All mommies have important jobs, they have so much to do.

But the job that mommies love the most is taking care of you!

ABOUT THE AUTHORS

Lauren and Michael Quick are a married couple living in the land of the Great Lakes. They enjoy sleeping in, long beach walks, and…

JUST KIDDING.

They have two boys, Asher (3) and Levi (1), that bring them great joy, in addition to early mornings and a messy house. They wouldn't have it any other way.

CPSIA information can be obtained
at www.ICGtesting.com
Printed in the USA
BVHW010727190821
614718BV00017B/129